This Igloo book belongs to

_ _

igloobooks
.com

Published in 2012
by Igloo Books Ltd
Cottage Farm
Sywell
Northants
NN6 0BJ
www.igloo-books.com

Original story by Igloo Books Ltd
Party Paws™ & A Little Bear Called Bamboo™
are registered Trade Marks of © Artworld Inspirations Limited

SHE001 0812
2 4 6 8 10 9 7 5 3 1
ISBN: 978-0-85780-659-8
Printed and manufactured in China

Santa Paws

igloobooks
.com

It's Christmas time and Bamboo
and his friends have lots to do.
They are busy getting things ready.

They write cards for all of their friends
and wrap lots of presents with big
bows and pretty paper.

Bamboo takes all his cards
and presents to the post office
and mails them to his friends.

Bamboo goes into the woods
and collects lots of flowers and mistletoe,
to make a pretty Christmas ring.

Bamboo hangs the ring on his front door.
What a pretty sight!

Bamboo and his friends search
for a big, Christmas tree.
They pick the best one and take it home.

They decorate the tree with lots of sparkly baubles and a shiny, red star.

Bamboo hangs his stocking over the fireplace
and puts milk and cookies out for Santa Paws.

When Bamboo and his friends are tucked up in bed, Santa Paws arrives with a sack of presents.

Santa Paws places the presents
under the Christmas tree for Bamboo
and his friends to find in the morning.

Finally, it's Christmas morning!
Bamboo wakes up full of excitement.

Santa Paws has left lots
of lovely treats and toys inside
Bamboo's stocking.

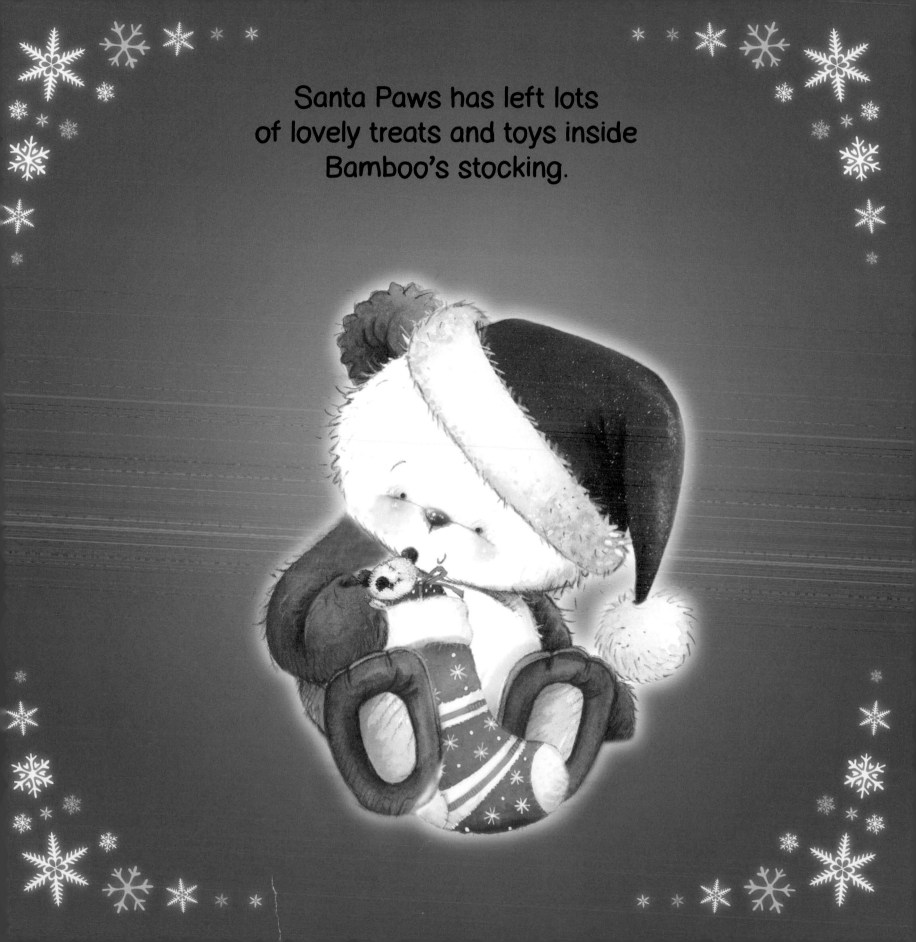

When Bamboo and his friends look out
of their windows, they see that it has snowed.
They run outside to make a snowbear.

Next, they play hide-and-seek.
Bamboo climbs up into a tree and sits
very still while his friends look for him.

Clouds gather in the sky and it begins to snow.
Bamboo and his friends jump with joy
and dance through the snowflakes.

In the glistening snow, they snuggle
together on a bench to keep warm.
Soon, it's time to go back inside.

Inside, Bamboo and his friends have
lots of cards and presents to open.
They take it in turns to give each other gifts.

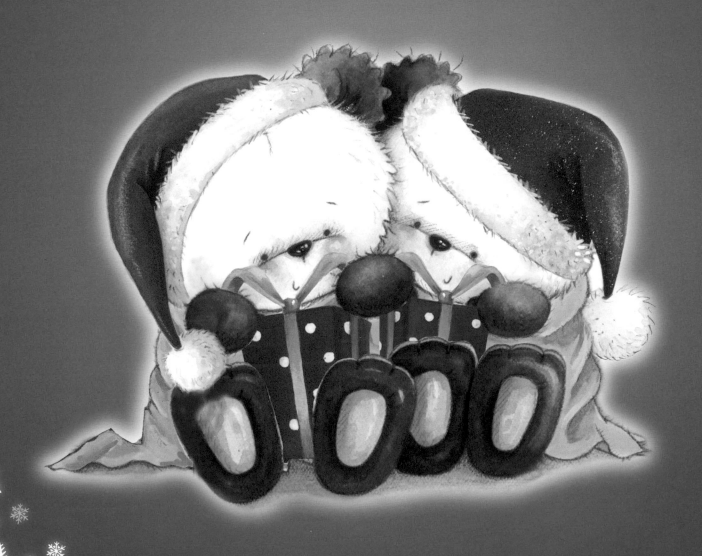

They find lots of lovely things
inside their presents.
There is something special for everyone.

Bamboo and his friends celebrate,
pulling crackers and
singing lots of Christmas songs.

They eat a delicious meal
and then snuggle down in front
of the fireplace with a cup of cocoa.

cocoa

cocoa

Bamboo and his friends have shared lots
of special memories together and
had lots of fun. What a wonderful Christmas!